This Book Belongs To:

_____

This book was printed by Taylor Specialty Books in Dallas, Texas, using soy-based inks. The paper includes 10% post consumer waste (PCW) recycled content. The paper is Forest Stewardship Council (FSC), Sustainable Forest Initiative (SFI), and Programme for the Endorsement of Forest Certification (PEFC) certified. The book parts meet or exceed all CPSIA guidelines for Pthalate Lead content.

TRAVELER

A STORY OF TRUST, FAITH, AND HOPE ENCIRCLED BY LOVE

Written by Mary Alice Parmley

Illustrated by Jackie Onstead

Indian Trail Press • Topeka, Kansas

TRAVELER: A STORY OF TRUST, FAITH, AND HOPE ENCIRCLED BY LOVE

Written by Mary Alice Parmley

Illustrated by Jackie Onstead

Text and illustrations ©2010 by Mary Alice Parmley

First Edition
Published 2011 by Indian Trail Press

Indian Trail Press

2241 SW Indian Trail
Topeka, Kansas 66614

www.mrsparmley.com   E-mail: contact@mrsparmley.com

Ordering Information:

Special discounts are available on quantity purchases by organizations, schools, and others. For details, contact the publisher at the address above.

Design by Fred Holmes. Text set in Mendoza. The illustrations in this book were produced with oil paints on a linen canvas.
Original artwork digitization by Arthur Brown.

Parmley, Mary Alice.
  Traveler : a story of trust, faith, and hope
encircled by love / written by Mary Alice Parmley ;
illustrated by Jackie Onstead. -- 1st ed.
  p. cm.
  SUMMARY: In this Christmas story, Traveler, a Beagle
dog, finds friendship and love from his new friends at
the inn and the stable where Jesus is born.
  Audience: Ages 2-9.
  ISBN-13: 978-0-9740159-2-7
  ISBN-10: 0-9740159-2-X

  1. Beagle (Dog breed)--Juvenile fiction.
  2. Friendship--Juvenile fiction. 3. Christmas stories.
  [1. Beagle (Dog breed)--Fiction. 2. Dogs--Fiction.
  3. Friendship--Fiction. 4. Christmas--Fiction.]
  I. Onstead, Jackie, ill. II. Title.

  PZ7.P2427Tra 2011   [E]
  QBI11-600148

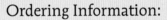

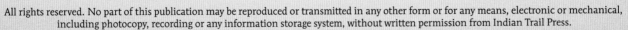

Foreword

Mary Alice Parmley has enjoyed reading good children's literature throughout her life. She used children's literature to teach important values and life's great adventures to her own daughter and all her classroom children.

She frequently lectures student teachers, administrators, and community groups on the gifts of teaching. She speaks on many educational subjects, including the importance of hugging young people, the need to read to children at an early age, and how a good teacher works as the "chairman of the board," leading students while being a good listener.

This beautifully illustrated storybook introduces children to the many gifts in life that come from friendship. Mrs. Parmley has always believed that "to have a friend you must be one." The Nativity story is the backdrop of Traveler's journey to Bethlehem where the ultimate gifts of friendship and love were born to mankind.

Dedication… *For the child in all of us.*

Traveler is a story of trust, faith, and hope encircled
by love. To my beloved family, many friends and kind
readers, I take great joy in knowing you will
embrace the blessings of the Nativity story
told from the perspective of a small Beagle
dog. Be encouraged every day that love
abounds in small packages.

M any years ago, a small dog was swept
along a dusty road on a far and fearful journey.

He was weary for he had traveled such a long, long way, as he tried to avoid the pounding hooves of the horseback riders.

Their voices shouted, "On to Bethlehem!" Chariot drivers urgently called out directions to reach this city in Judea. None of the shouting meant a thing to one small weary dog, though he knew he must follow this rowdy crowd to find a place where he could rest.

He paused at an inn and thought, "This might be a place to stop for rest." Then he heard the Innkeeper call to his wife, "Look, Mother, we have a visitor!"

"Are you a lost puppy in need of some place to stay?" inquired the Innkeeper's wife. "You must be hungry. You look so weary and your paw is hurt!" He was tired and hungry, but he thumped his tail against the doorway of the inn. "Let me bring you some food, little traveler, and we can take a look at your hurt paw" said the Innkeeper's wife.

"I'll tie it up in a soft cloth," said the Innkeeper. "And I think you need a name! I'm going to name you Traveler," the Innkeeper's wife said.

As the little dog ate, the Innkeeper agreed, "I think 'Traveler' is just the right name for him! I think you need a place to stay little Traveler; you can stay with us." The Innkeeper's wife said, "Our stable would be a warm place for you to sleep."

Traveler followed along behind the Innkeeper to the stable where he saw a baby lying in a manger bed of clean, sweet-smelling hay. The Innkeeper said to the baby's parents, "We have another weary traveler, and I think he would like to stay with you."

The people, whom the Innkeeper called Mary and Joseph, welcomed him. Mary spoke softly to Traveler and said, "Yes, we can always use another pair of bright eyes to watch over us."

Traveler snuggled close to Mary, and she welcomed him to be with her family. She cradled her baby, called Jesus, and Traveler laid his soft brown and white head in her lap next to the baby boy. Traveler had a special feeling for this new baby and his mother. With one soft paw, he touched the mother and baby. Traveler was trying to say, "I'll help you with the little one."

Something just told him this would be a special night where he was needed. A warmth and peace settled throughout the walls of the small stable bringing comfort to the stablemates—Mary's faithful donkey, a mother cat, and her kittens.

A bright light was spreading over his new-found world! Visitors were following this bright light in the sky that beamed down on the stable. The first visitors were shepherds. Traveler knew this because he heard Joseph tell Mary, "The shepherds are here!"

They wore long cloaks and carried staffs. Some of the shepherds carried little lambs.
Traveler watched the shepherds as they came closer to see the baby.

The days passed, healing
Traveler's hurt paw and bringing
more visitors. Wise men, who
had traveled from afar, brought
gifts of gold, frankincense,
and myrrh.

They knelt down to worship this blessed Christ Child. Traveler kept close watch over the family and their many visitors honoring the newborn baby.

There came a day when Traveler noticed Mary and the baby being helped onto their donkey. "Was the family leaving?" questioned Traveler.

Traveler stood close
to his Innkeeper friends
as he watched the baby
he loved and his parents
moving along. The
Innkeeper looked down
at his sad friend and said,
"It's alright, Traveler.
You go along.
Every little boy needs a dog."

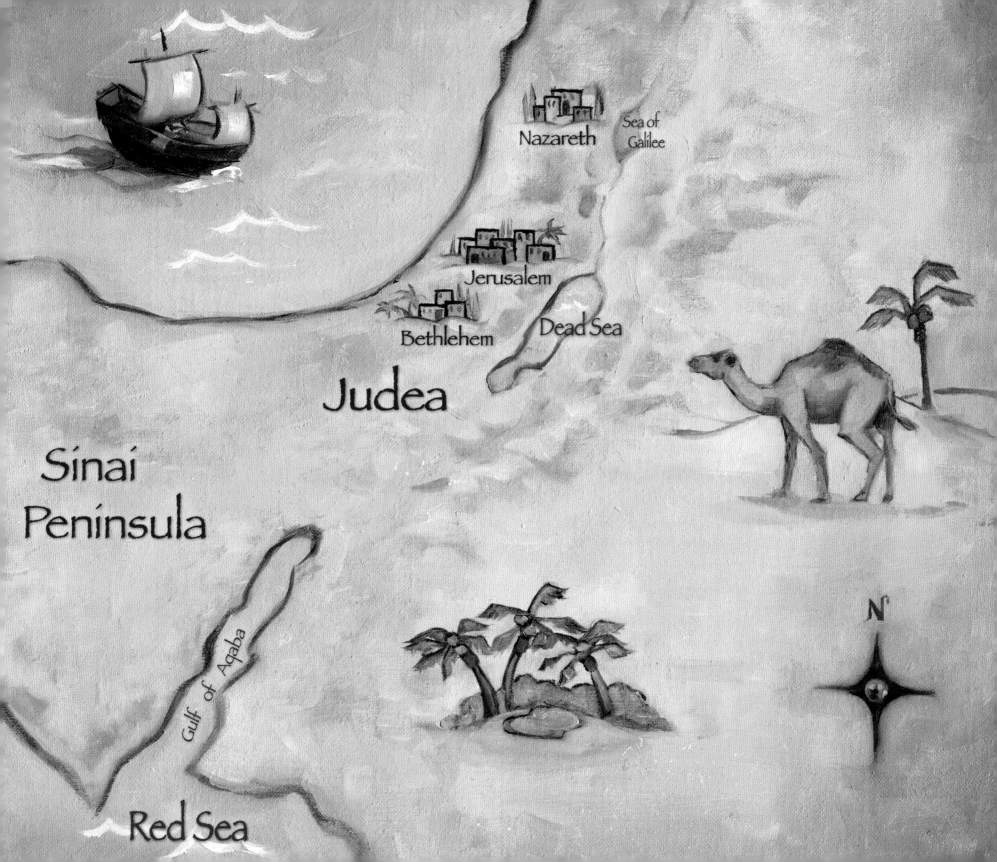

Let's Talk About the Story

What is the name of the city called out by the chariot drivers?

What is the dog's name in the story?

What is the name of the baby in the story?

What is the reason Traveler gets his name?

What kind of dog is Traveler?

What kindnesses do the Innkeeper and his wife show Traveler?

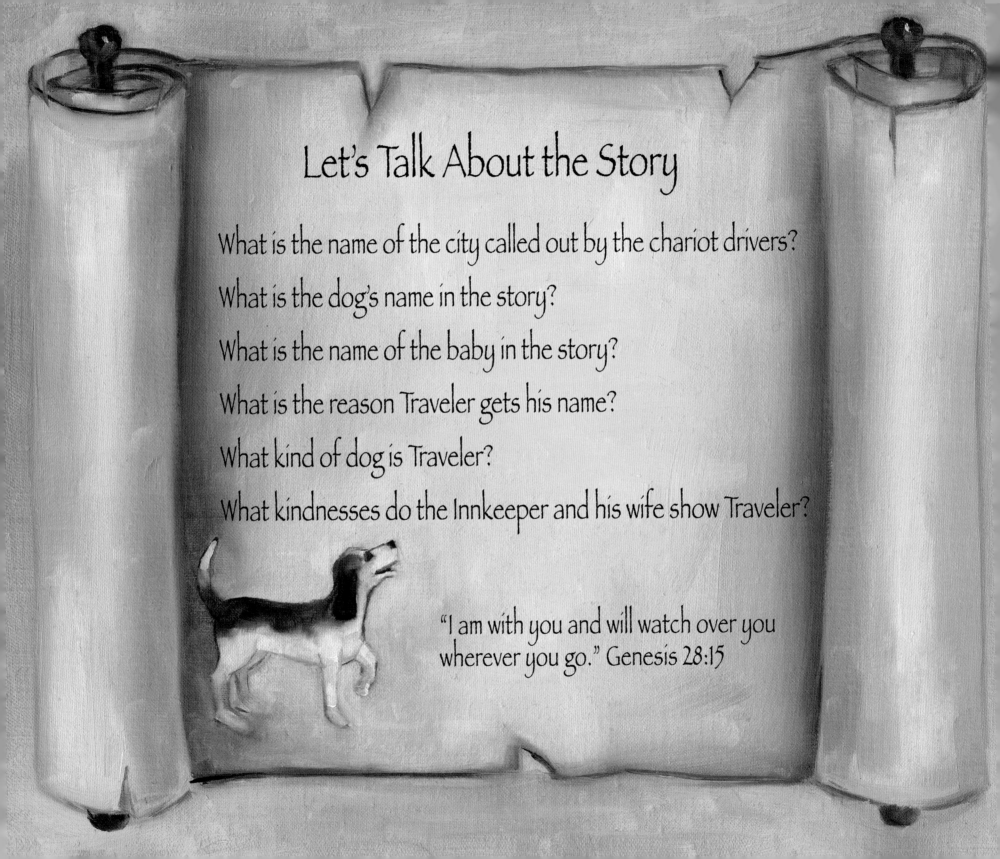

"I am with you and will watch over you wherever you go." Genesis 28:15

Let's Talk About the Story

What is up in the sky guiding the visitors to the stable?

Who comes to visit baby Jesus?

What do the visitors bring to show their love for baby Jesus?

How does Traveler show his love for his new friends?

What holiday do we celebrate because of the birth of Jesus?

How many days until Christmas?

"The Lord will guide you continually."
Isaiah 58:11

Mary Alice Parmley, Author

Mary Alice Parmley is known and loved as a teacher of children and adults who are children at heart. Author of *Seasons, Thoughtful Reflection in Poetry,* she has written poems and children's stories her entire life. She began creating heartfelt, inspiring stories in her hometown of Marion, Kansas, which is nestled in the rolling Flint Hills. Through the years she was encouraged to write "just one more story" by her daughter, Mary Ann, as well as her many students.

During her forty-four-year career as a master teacher, she knew the importance of showing encouragement and respect, giving of herself to others, and lending a hand through friendship. By example, she conveyed these values to her students.

As a retired teacher in Topeka, Kansas, she inspires others with her passion for life. She enjoys volunteering, especially as a storyteller, and is active in the community.

Parmley believes that a good, caring teacher can have tremendous impact on a child. Her teaching style and unique knowledge of what children love inspired her to write *Traveler.* Learn more about Parmley and *Traveler* at www.mrsparmley.com.

Jackie Onstead, Illustrator

Jackie Onstead grew up in Sioux Falls, South Dakota. Her love of art began at an early age and was encouraged by her artistic mother. As a child, she loved to look at illustrations in children's books and filled sketchbooks with doodles and drawings of her own.

While pursuing a master's degree in commercial art, she was introduced to painting with oils, which has remained her favorite medium. Good stories, with heart, provide her inspiration to illustrate and *Traveler* did just that. Jackie and her husband Brian live in Omaha, Nebraska.

For more fun with Traveler and the latest product information, please visit:

www.mrsparmley.com